WHAT'S FOR DINNER, MR GUM?

Andy Stanton

Illustrated by David Tazzyman

First published 2009
by Egmont UK Limited
This Large Print edition published by
AudioGO Ltd
by arrangement with
Egmont UK Limited 2011

ISBN: 978 1405 664677

British Library Cataloguing in Publication Data

Printed and bound in Great Britain by
MPG Books Group Limited

For Andy, Kathy and Ellie
And for Bob, the fattest cat in L.A.

CONTENTS

SOME OF THE CRAZY OLD TOWNSFOLK FROM LAMONIC BIBBER

Mrs Lovely

Friday O'Leary

Billy William the Third

Old Granny

Mr Gum

Martin Launderette

Alan Taylor

Polly

CHAPTER ONE

OFF TO THE SEASIDE!

This is the story of the Battle of Lamonic Bibber, or as it became known, the Dinnertime Wars or, as it didn't become known, *Ghostbusters III*. And know this, my friends—it was a terrible conflict indeed. Like all wars it was full of madness and anger. Like all wars there were courageous heroes and dastardly villains. Like *practically* all wars there was a dirty little monkey called Philip the Horror.

But I know what you're wondering. You're wondering how the Dinnertime Wars got started in the first place, aren't you?

'How did it all start?' you say.

'Where did it begin?' you ask.

'What do you mean, a monkey?' you enquire.

'Shut up,' I reply. 'Stop bothering me

with all these questions and I will tell you.'

*   *   *

It all started on a Friday. And not only did it start on a Friday but it started *with* a Friday—that wonderful old gentleman Friday O'Leary, hero of many an adventure and three times winner of the Lamonic Bibber Women's Underwater Badminton Championship.

And here's a quick word from Friday himself:

'BREADBIN'

Thanks, Friday.

But hey now, hey now, don't dream it's over. This story doesn't just start with Friday O'Leary. Because along with him were his good friends Polly and Alan Taylor.

Now, Polly was a little girl with the sort of sandy-coloured hair that makes you happy to be alive and the sort of heart-coloured heart which is so brave

2

it would fight a lion if that lion happened to deserve it. For instance, if he had been trying to rob pencils. Polly was only nine but she was a hero through and through.

And as for Alan Taylor, he was a gingerbread man with electric muscles and he was 16.24cm tall because he'd grown a centimetre since the last book he was in.

'Maybe I'll grow into a real man one day,' he was fond of saying. But that was impossible.

Or *was* it?

Yes.

But never mind. For the most part, Alan Taylor was a jolly little twinkle and girls liked him because he was cute and they could dress him up like a doll and make him do tea parties.

'Oh, you are a darlin' little marshy,' laughed Polly now, bending down to kiss Alan Taylor on his juicy raisin eye. 'An' this is gonna be the best holiday ever!'

'That's right,' laughed Friday O'Leary, throwing his hat up in the air. It landed on a cloud and the cloud laughed so hard it turned into a lovely apple. 'We're off to the seaside and we won't be back for weeks!'

'Hoorays!' said Polly.

'Huzzooof!' said Alan Taylor.

'THE TRUTH IS A LEMON MERINGUE!' yelled Friday, as he sometimes liked to do. 'It's seaside time for us!'

And off they toddled down the friendly road and the sun shone down and the trees were brown and there wasn't a frown in the whole wide world, just Friday, a biscuit and a happy little girl.

CHAPTER TWO

BUTCHER SHOP BLUES

Deep inside Billy William the Third's Right Royal Meats someone stood in the dismal shadows, watching the heroes go. It was that appalling butcher, Billy William the Third.

'Ha ha ha,' grinned Billy now. 'With them lot of do-gooders gone down the seaside to do their sunbathin' an' their sandcastles, the way is clear for evil. For once me an' me old pal Mr Gum'll be free to do our plans in peace. An' then we'll RULE this stupid town!'

And that's how it went in Lamonic Bibber. Billy William and Mr Gum were always trying to hatch their scoundrel plans and the heroes were always squashing them back down.

So it was no wonder that seeing Polly and her friends leaving town put Billy in a good evil mood.

No more heroes any more!

he sang.

No more heroes any more!
They walked right past me butcher's door!
Now me an' Mr Gum's gonna rule the roost!
What's a roost, I don't even know?
But who even cares, cos the heroes are gone!
An' now I'm gonna sing me song!
Yeah yeah yeah yeah, nothin' can stop us!
Not even an interferin' diplodocus.

As Billy sang he beat out a rhythm on the counter with a pair of chicken drumsticks. He closed his eyes and pretended he was a rock star guy called Space Age Billy and the Meat Brigade.

No more heroes any more!

They walked right past me butcher's door!

Me name is Space Age Billy, I'm a funky man!

He was Number 1 in the charts and all the girls fancied him. He was the best!

But hang on. Just where *was* Mr Gum exactly?

Billy opened his eyes and snapped back to reality. He must have been singing for hours. It was getting dark outside. An owl flew past the window. Then another owl flew past. Then Dracula and his friend Clive walked by on their way to the pub. It was night time—but still no Mr Gum.

'That's funty,' said Billy. (You see, that was how Billy William pronounced the word 'funny'.) 'Mr Gum always comes here for his Friday night dinner. He loves feastin' on the entrails an' stale burgers what I feed him. In all these years he ain't never once been late.'

Billy's pet flies buzzed around his head, picking at the tiny morsels of meat he kept in his ears for their treats.

The clock on the wall ticked.

Billy waited patiently, but inside his heart was slowly sinking like a battle ship. Until finally he had to admit it. Mr Gum wasn't going to show.

'Well, that's it. I can't wait no longer,' yawned Billy, his butcher's cap drooping wearily in the gloom. 'There's nothin' for it but to shut up shop an' call it a night.'

*   *   *

'I don't get it,' said Billy as he tucked himself into his freezing cold bed. 'A whole town to muck up an' no Mr Gum to muck it up with! It ain't no fun doin' plans on me own.'

Billy looked up at the poster on the wall. It was his secret joy. It was a pin-up of Thora Gruntwinkle, the Butcher Queen of Olde London Town. She was holding a meat cleaver dripping with guts.

'Imagine if you an' me was married, Thora me darlin',' said Billy. 'Then I wouldn't be lonely no more. An' I

13

wouldn't need no Mr Gum neither,' he added spitefully.

Billy blew out his bedside candle and soon he was fast asleep, sucking his thumb and dreaming of punting downstream with Thora Gruntwinkle at his side, feeding her chicken livers and gently stroking her long red fingernails.

Chapter Three

BILLY ON THE TRAIL

Another lonely night down at the butcher's. The flies buzzed lazily through the murk. Billy sat with his feet on the counter, staring up at the clock.

Seven o'clock.

Seven thirty.

Eight o'clock.

If only I could tell the time, thought Billy. *Then at least there'd be some point starin' up at the clock.*

But he couldn't. AND THAT'S WHAT HAPPENS IF YOU BUNK OFF SCHOOL LIKE BILLY, SO WATCH IT.

'Well,' sighed Billy as the evening wore on. 'Looks like Mr Gum ain't comin' in tonight neither, the lousy stinkin'—hey, there he is!' he cried suddenly. 'Me best pal in the whole world what I'd never say a bad word about! He's back!'

And yes! There was Mr Gum now,

15

creeping along the high street in his hobnail boots. His big red beard blazed like a beacon in the twilight. His bloodshot eyes darted cunningly around, looking for trouble. His dusty jacket flapped out behind him like a bad wizard's cloak. And he was licking his lips greedily. He wanted the scoffs.

'An' I'm the one to give him them scoffs,' grinned Billy. 'I'm gonna feed him up like a champion! Everythin's back to normal.'

But that's where Billy was wrong. Mr Gum walked straight past Billy William the Third's Right Royal Meats. He crossed over the road, kicked a beer can at a nightingale, and disappeared round the corner.

Billy did a thought. Then, without a second thought, he slunk out of the butcher's shop. Taking care to keep to the shadows and to not yell out things like, 'HEY, MR GUM! I'M FOLLOWING YOU!' Billy crept after his horrible old pal.

'Shabba me whiskers!' he heard Mr Gum mutter up ahead. 'I'm gonna be late for me dinner!'

Oho! Billy nodded to himself. 'Late for dinner is it? I knew he was up to something! But what? It's a mittersy.' (You see, that was how Billy William pronounced the word 'mystery'.)

Mr Gum picked his way through the quiet streets, his hobnail boots clomp-clomp-clompin' on the cobblestones. And behind him rode Billy William ~~on his magic unicorn, Elizabeth~~.

'Hang on,' frowned Billy. 'I ain't got no ~~magic unicorn called Elizabeth~~.'

Mr Gum picked his way through the quiet streets, his hobnail boots clomp-clomp-clompin' on the cobblestones. And behind him crept Billy William. There were no ~~magic unicorns~~ in sight.

*   *   *

By now Mr Gum had come to the stone steps that led down to the old canal. Mr Gum did a big crafty look and went tiptoeing down the slimy steps. Billy did an even bigger crafty look and went tiptoeing after him. Mr Gum did an ENORMOUS crafty look and went tiptoeing along the canal towpath. Billy did an even BIGGER crafty look which was so large it didn't even fit on his face. But somehow he managed it because that's how determined he was to look craftier than Mr Gum.

The two bad men tiptoed along the canal, the dirty water lapping softly in the evening breeze. Many years ago the canal had been a glorious waterway, transporting over 90% of all England's emails down to Cornwall. But in these modern times all the email transportation was done over the Internet and no one used the canal any more, except to dump shopping trolleys in. The water was brown and useless. If you drank it you would die and I should know because I drank it once and I died.

But now a new smell came to Billy William's long nose above the stench of the stagnant, brown water. It was the smell of old cooking oil and chip fat. And suddenly a cold chill passed over him as he realised where Mr Gum was headed.

19

'No,' whispered Billy. 'It couldn't be ... It's too upsettin' to even imagine ...'

But there it was. A fizzing neon sign, which blinked and buzzed in the darkness like a sinister fig.

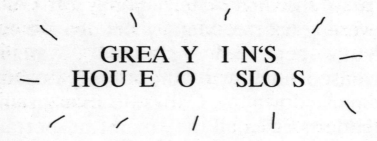

GREA Y I N'S
HOU E O   SLO S

CHAPTER FOUR

GREASY IAN'S HOUSE OF SLOPS

'No,' whispered Billy as Mr Gum approached the buzzing neon sign. Despite what he was seeing, Billy prayed he was wrong. Surely Mr Gum wasn't really going to eat his dinner elsewhere? Surely he wasn't really going to eat at the dirtiest kebab shop known to man or beast—Greasy Ian's House of Slops.

Billy watched as Mr Gum stole one last glance around him. Then swift as a crab, the sneaky old beardy crawled in through a little cat flap set into the rusted metal door. Billy crept up to the window as close as he dared. He had to know for sure.

'Oi! Greasy Ian!' Mr Gum was yelling now. 'I wants me dinner an' I wants it quick smart!'

Billy looked on as the man behind the counter turned slowly around. He was a terrifying bulk of a fellow with

21

boils all over his face and brains. There was a long scar on his left arm from his days as a barbed-wire salesman and one of his hands was made of brass after a terrible accident involving a chainsaw, some superglue and a brass hand.

'Mr Gum,' grinned Greasy Ian, beads of sweat rolling down his blotchy purple face. 'I knew ye'd be back. Once ye've had one o' ma doner kebabs ye're hooked for life!'

'It's true, Greasy Ian,' laughed Mr Gum. 'I been thinkin' 'bout 'em all week. The meat, the sauce, them little polystyrene boxes you puts 'em in what ruins up the environment—it's drivin' me mad an' I gotta have more! MORE! MORE! MORE! LESS! I mean, MORE!'

'Well, yer in luck, ye big dribblin' demon,' leered Greasy Ian. 'I'm cookin' up a storm tonight! So what'll it be? The usual, aye?'

'Aye,' agreed Mr Gum. 'A blimmin' enormous kebab drippin' with tons of grey sauce so it goes all over me clothes.'

'Comin' right up, ' said Greasy Ian. He twirled his carving knife and began hacking into the enormous slab of meat that was turning slowly on the spit behind him.

And who was turning the spit? Yes. It was that monkey I told you about earlier.

'Philip the Horror!' gasped Billy William outside. 'So the rumours were true—he really does exist!'

And what a dreadful little beast that monkey was. His eyes were filled with a terrible intelligence which was almost human and his tail was filled with whatever monkey's tails are filled with. He wore a scrappy little t-shirt but no trousers because he enjoyed letting his little farts out so much and, as he turned the spit, he jumped up and down, chattering in the Language of the Monkeys.

'Faster!' growled Greasy Ian as he sheared off long, grey, curly strips of meat. 'Faster, Philip, faster!'

'CHATTER! CHATTER! CHATTER!' cried Philip the Horror as he turned the handle, faster and faster and faster yet. 'CHATTER! CHATTER! CHEE!'

And as Billy William gazed through the window, great billows of steam rose in the shop and Greasy Ian's face was grinning through the haze, and the flames rose higher and the meat whizzed round and the flames rose higher and the meat whizzed round and the flames rose higher and the meat whizzed round, round and around and aroooooouuuuuunddddd . . .

🐾 🐾 🐾

The meat turned round and the monkey chattered!

Down at Greasy Ian's that was all that mattered!

The monkey chattered and the meat turned round!

And Mr Gum laughed to hear that sound!

And the chip fat bubbled and the night
was on fire

With Mr G's kebab desire!

And the night was on fire and the
chip fat bubbled!

And Billy's vision blurred and doubled!

CHIP CHIP CHIP!

CHOP! CHOP! CHOP!

Down at Greasy Ian's House of Slops!

CHATTER CHATTER CHATTER!

CHATTER CHATTER CHEE!

Just like hell, where the Devil be!

SLASH SLASH SLASH!

SLICE SLICE SLICE!

Greasy Ian's carving knife!

CHATTER CHATTER CHATTER!

CHATTER CHATTER CHEE!

Mr Gum, Greasy Ian and the monkey

makes three!

The knife's blade flashed and the meat

was sliced!

And carved and halved and chopped

and diced!

The meat was sliced and the knife's

blade flashed!

And the pots they clattered and

crashed and bashed!

And the walls were dripping and the chips were hot

Greasy Ian did a poo in the cooking pot!

And the chips were hot and the walls were dripping

And Philip the Horror was dancing and skipping!

BASH BASH BASH!

BAM BAM BAM!

Greasy Ian carving up the lamb!

CHATTER CHATTER CHATTER!

CHATTER CHATTER CHEE!

And they danced in the flames,

so wild and free!

FLICKER FLICKER FLICKER!

FLAME FLAME FLAME!

Kebabs were Greasy Ian's game!

CHATTER CHATTER CHATTER!

CHATTER CHATTER CHEE!

Just like hell, where the Devil be!

*　　*　　*

Finally the terrifying display of cooking was at an end. Philip the Horror eased up on the handle and gradually the column of spinning meat slowed down, coming to a stop with a soft, squelchy *PPPPPPHFFFFT TTTHHHHTTTT*.

'There ye go, pally,' said Greasy Ian, slapping the kebab into something that was either a bit of pita bread or an oven glove, it was impossible to tell.

'Delicious,' mumbled Mr Gum, big gobs of sauce squirting out the side of the kebab and running down his beard in a thick juicy stream.

'I never seen him lookin' so happy,' thought Billy. 'Never once in all these years.'

'Mmmmph! Scoffle! Yub!' snorted Mr Gum, cramming the last of the kebab down his throat. 'What a taste! Much better than Billy's borin' old entrails!'

Outside, Billy clutched his heart as if wounded by a dagger with 'DISLOYALTY' written on the handle.

'What?' said Greasy Ian. 'Ye're not still hangin' 'round with that butcher fella, are ye?'

'Nah, I don't need Billy no more,' laughed Mr Gum, talking WITH HIS MOUTH FULL. 'Not now I got you, me old grizzler!'

'That's right,' chuckled Greasy Ian. 'Ye don't need to hang around with losers like Billy when ye can hang 'round with losers like me an' Philip the Horror! We're yer best friends now, aye?'

'Aye,' said Mr Gum and then the two of them were laughing together through the smoke and the steam and Philip the Horror was hooting and clapping his monkey paws together and that was it. Billy couldn't stand it a second longer.

He pushed open the cat flap and burst into the kebab shop ~~on his magic unicorn, Elizabeth~~.

'BILLY!' cried Mr Gum, hastily wiping his beard on his sleeve. 'What you doin' here?'

'The question is what YOU doin' here, Mr Gum?' cried Billy. 'You gone

36

an' found yourself another scoff merchant, haven't you! HAVEN'T YOU!'

'No, I never!' protested Mr Gum. 'It ain't how it looks, Billy! You gone out your mind with jealous thoughts!'

'Forget it,' sobbed Billy. 'I seen it all. You scoffed that kebab down like a common werewolf! I seen it all an' I heard it all an' I smelt it all! I'm sick of you an' your lies, Mr Gum! You ain't nothin' but a cheatin', deceitful, pinched-up little scooper!'

'But—but—but,' started Mr Gum.

'No buts,' said Billy. He pointed a trembling finger towards Greasy Ian and Philip the Horror. 'You got your new mates now. Well, I hope the three of you's gonna be very happy together!'

And with that Billy William dived back through the cat flap and took off into the night, hardly knowing where he was going and hardly caring that he didn't know and hardly even caring that he didn't care that he didn't know.

'CHATTER! CHATTER! CHATTER!'
Philip the Horror's shrieks chased Billy all the way along the canal, echoing off the flagstones.
'CHATTER CHATTER CHEEEEEEE!'

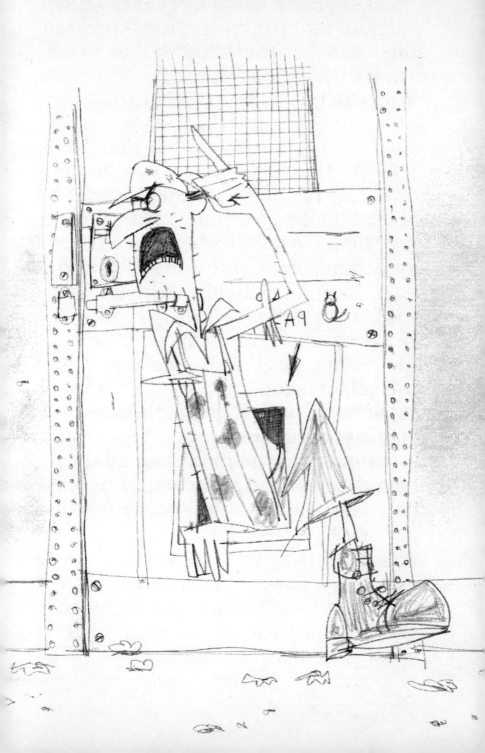

CHAPTER FIVE

BILLY SOWS THE SEEDS
OF HIS REVENGE

I never thought I'd say it, but poor old Billy. All night long he tossed and turned in his freezing cold bed, his gruesome little head a-spinnin' and a-sparkin' with the terrible things he'd seen and heard. Greasy Ian's wild sweaty face . . . Philip the Horror's gut-wrenching squeals . . . Mr Gum's jaws swooping down into the kebab meat . . .

'NOOO!' yelled Billy, throwing his blanket to the floor.

Thora Gruntwinkle looked down from her place on the wall, but what help was she? She was mere ink and paper. The real Thora Gruntwinkle was all the way down in Olde London Town, probably kissing some big handsome sailor right now. Or a guy with loads of money. Or a bloke who occasionally washed. Why

40

would she want a loser like Billy?

'I'M ALONE!' howled Billy. 'ALOOOOOOONE!'

As the night wore on, Billy's thoughts grew darker and darker still.

'It's all Mr Gum's fault,' he growled. 'He's the one what deserted me.'

Mr Gum it's his fault Deserted
Deserted Fault Breadbin Mr Gum

The words went spinning around and around in Billy's mind until finally one dreadful word repeated itself over and over in huge blood-red letters:

RIVINGE

(You see, that was how Billy William pronounced the word 'revenge'.)

'I'll show Mr Gum he can't go 'round gettin' new pals an' leavin' me all

alone,' he vowed. 'But how? I wish I was a shark, then he'd be sorry. I'd lie in the ocean waitin' for him to go on holiday an' then—SNAP! That'd learn him.'

But Billy had to face it—he wasn't a shark. Not even a little one.

Finally, as dawn was breaking, an idea came to him.

'That's it!' exclaimed Billy William. 'I ain't a shark, I'm a genius. A blibberin' genius! But I'm gonna need three things—some seeds, some more seeds an' a few more seeds jus' to make sure.'

*   *   *

ONE WEEK LATER . . .

Mr Gum was sitting out in his garden, relaxing in his favourite broken deckchair and reading a copy of *The History of Kebabs*, which Greasy Ian had lent him. Mr Gum hated reading but he liked the pictures. One of the pictures showed a small boy crying because he'd eaten too much chilli

43

sauce. Another showed a vegetarian being attacked by doner kebabs. It made Mr Gum laugh.

The sun was shining merrily in the sky and the birds and squirrels were playing happily in the trees. But despite all this Mr Gum was in a good mood.

'Mmmm,' he said, licking some old sauce off one of the pages. But then he noticed something. Something on the lawn. Something yellow and green and . . .

Mr Gum's tongue stopped mid-lick.

He looked around.

Come to think of it, the garden was full of the things.

Dozens of them.

Hundreds of them.

'SHABBA ME WHISKERS!' yelled Mr Gum, jumping out of his deckchair like a horrid stallion. 'SHABBA ME KEBAB-CHOMPIN' WHISKERS!'

Mr Gum's lawn was infested with hundreds and hundreds of his old enemies—corn on the cob.

Mr Gum couldn't stand corn on the cob. Mr Gum hated corn on the cob. You know how kryptonite makes Superman throw up all over his cape and go really weak? That's almost what it was like with Mr Gum and corn on the cob.

'Yisp!' he moaned feebly, falling to the ground. 'Throob! Vastrich! Prut! I can't bears it! I can't stands it! I can't

takes it! I can't endures it! I can't stomachs it! I can't helps it! I don't LIKES it!'

Mr Gum began crawling towards the

house. His head was swimming and his stomach felt like it was playing table tennis against a Womble.

'Gotta . . . keep . . . goin' . . . ' he gasped. 'Gotta . . . get . . . away.'

Eventually he made it inside and up to his dirty bedroom where he lay panting on his unmade bed. When he had finally recovered he risked a look out the broken window and suddenly all the strength and fury rushed back into his body.

The corn on the cobs had been planted to spell out a message.

NO ONE MESSES WITH BILLY WILLIAM THE THIRD!

'WHO DID THIS?!' screamed Mr Gum. Then he realised it was probably Billy William the Third.

'That's right, you appallin' snocklehead!' called Billy at that precise moment, sticking his nose over Mr Gum's garden fence.

'I planted 'em—an' why? To get me rivinge!! You ain't me friend no more,

Mr Gum! Just consider yourself lucky I ain't a shark!'

And off he tore down the road ~~on his magic unicorn, Elizabeth,~~ laughing, laughing, laughing.

'I'LL GET YOU!' said Mr Gum in capital letters. 'Just you wait, Billy me boy! Just you wait an' see!'

CHAPTER SIX

THE INCIDENT OF BILLY AND THE FLIES

That crafty old Gumster waited 'til the sun had set and—

THUD!

Night had fallen. Then off he skiffled to Billy William the Third's Right Royal Meats.

Carefully he hid himself outside the butcher's shop and lay in wait. Where did he hide? I don't know, because he was hidden.

Eventually the lights in the butcher's shop went off. Soon after, there came the sound of Billy's snoring: 'YYY'. (You see that was how Billy William pronounced 'ZZZ'.)

Mr Gum tiptoed over to the shop door on his hands and knees. Then he took a large cardboard box from under his hat. He took off the lid and poured

49

the contents through the letterbox.

'Feast well, me little leggities,' whispered Mr Gum, his eyes blazing in the darkness. It was starting to rain but Mr Gum didn't care. He liked the rain. It proved that evil was afoot.

*   *   *

The next morning Billy got up. Like every morning he gave the poster of Thora Gruntwinkle a delicate little kiss.

Like every morning he shuffled into the bathroom to stick extra stubble on his chin and to unbrush his teeth.

And like every morning, he went downstairs to feed the hundreds of pet flies who lived in his shop.

'Who wants some grub?' Billy called to his pets as he ladled heaps of slimy entrails into a big black bucket. 'Henry? Lisa? Wendy? Come an' get yer breakfast!'

But the familiar buzzing sound was not to be heard. The butcher's shop was eerily quiet.

'Where you all hidin'?' laughed Billy.

'Jasper? Vernon? Uncle Wing? Bunk? McNulty?'

Silence.

'Jolliper? Kenton? Crowdaddy? Stan? Nora? Oliver? Bluetail?' called Billy, desperately ladling the entrails into the bucket. He was starting to sweat. Something was wrong.

A single fly crawled weakly towards Billy across the dirty sawdust floor. It was Billy's favourite of them all—a tiny fellow called Little Billy.

'But jus' look at you!' cried Billy William. The ladle dropped from his hands and clattered into the bucket. 'Little Billy! Little Billy! What's happened to you?'

Billy William leaned forward to gather the poor little fly into his arms. One of Little Billy's legs was missing and his beautiful tiny eyes were shiny with fear.

Help me! he seemed to say as he staggered forward to Billy William, who was like the father he had never had. *Help me!*

But before Billy could take the stricken insect in his arms, the floor

51

started to heave and rumble. And suddenly an army of fat brown spiders who had been lying hidden in the sawdust reared up and pounced upon Little Billy.

The tiny fly fought with all his might. He fought with the strength of ten flies. But unfortunately the thirty-eight spiders fought with the strength of thirty-eight spiders. He didn't stand a chance.

And now Billy knew where all his other flies had gone. He fell to his knees and sobbed.

'WHYYYYY?' he wailed. 'WHYYYYYYYY?'

Outside the rain was falling, falling like Billy's own teardrops as he lay there in the sawdust. And the wind it blew as cold as the cold, cold feeling in Billy's heart. And three faces stood outside in the rain and the wind, smiling grimly through it all.

'Them spiders worked a treat,' growled Mr Gum as Philip the Horror gathered them back into the box to eat later.

'Aye,' said Greasy Ian, the raindrops slipping slickly off his oily hair.

'CHATTER! CHATTER! CHATTER!' shrieked Philip the Horror, jumping furiously up and down in the puddles. In each of his bright little eyes was reflected the pathetic figure of Billy William, sobbing into the sawdust. 'CHATTER! CHATTER! CHEE!'

CHAPTER SEVEN

THE DINNERTIME WARS

And now do you see how the tiniest disagreements spiral out of control? Do you? Do you? DO YOU REALLY? DO YOU? OH REALLY? DO YOU? DO YOU REALLY?

Well, OK then.

You see, just as the tiny acorn must one day grow into the mighty elephant, Mr Gum and Billy's fight had grown bigger and bigger by the hour. And the Incident of Billy and the Flies had pushed it over the edge. It was

W-A-R.

And that spells trouble.

So hide your heads in shame, my friends. For Lamonic Bibber's darkest days were now upon it.

The Dinnertime Wars had begun.

KA-BOOOOOOOOM!

Entrails and kebab scrapings flew
through the skies as Mr Gum and his
new pals slugged it out with Billy
William the Third.

KA-BLLLLAAAAAAAM!

Pig skulls and sheep bones littered
the war-torn ground. The streets ran
red with chilli sauce.

KA-BLUUUUUURRRRM!

A news reporter tried to sneak in with a helicopter but Greasy Ian got him with a pickled egg right between the eyes and he went home and cried to his mum.

KA-BLIMMMMMO!

By day the sun was hidden behind clouds of oily smoke. By night the sun was hidden because it was night-time. The townsfolk hid in their houses and the days grew dark, for that ghastly demon WAR stalked the earth, my friends. WAR, WAR, WAR!

*　　*　　*

The entrails soared and the fat it spattered!

In the Dinnertime Wars that was all

that mattered!

The fat it spattered and the entrails

soared!

As the demon of WAR it rumbled and

roared!

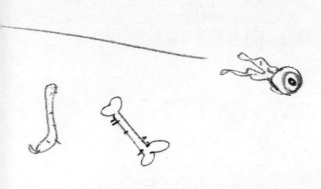

BOOM BOOM BOOM!

BANG BANG BANG!

Billy fighting the Kebab Shop Gang!

CHATTER CHATTER CHATTER!

CHATTER CHATTER CHEE!

Just like hell where the Devil be!

FIRE FIRE FIRE!

FAT FAT FAT!

One of Billy's burgers hit a passing cat!

CHATTER CHATTER CHATTER!

CHATTER CHATTER CHEE!

Three against one and one against three!

And the fighting flared and the sky turned black!

Greasy Ian accidentally kicked his monkey in the back!

And the sky turned black and the fighting flared!

And the people of the town were running scared!

WAR WAR WAR!

WOO WOO WOO!

Run, Billy run, they're after you!

CHATTER CHATTER CHATTER!

CHATTER CHATTER CHEE!

Mr Gum squirting sauce at a sycamore tree!

BUBBLE BUBBLE BUBBLE!

BOIL BOIL BOIL!

Greasy Ian, slopping out the oil!

CHATTER CHATTER CHATTER!

CHATTER CHATTER –

'NO! Not that monkey again!' cried Martin Launderette, who ran the launderette. 'I can't take it anymore!'

Big fat Jonathan Ripples ducked as a chicken carcass came hurtling by.

'I used to dream about flying food!' he trembled. 'But not like this!'

'Innocent people are getting hurt!' cried innocent people. 'Ouch!'

KA-BOOOOOOOM!

Billy launched a frozen turkey high into the air.

KA-BAAAAAAAB!

Greasy Ian rumbled a drum of flaming chip fat down the high street.

KA-LAAAAAUUUUUGH!

Mr Gum's insane laugh echoed off the gravy-splattered buildings.

'I've lived through eight World Wars,' declared Old Granny, taking a sip from the bottle of sherry she always kept hidden in her hair. 'But I've never seen anything as bad as this. We've got to get out of town!'

The townsfolk huddled in their houses, awaiting their chance to escape. And all around them the meat threw thick and fast.

KA-BOOM!

KA-BLAM!

KA-END OF CHAPTER!

CHAPTER EIGHT

THE HEROES RETURN

Friday O'Leary looked at the calendar he always wore around his neck. 'Well,' he said, 'we've been at the seaside for days now. Do you think it's time to go home yet?'

'Yeah,' said Polly. 'Let's go homes to good old Lamonic Bibber an' see what's been happenin' while we been away.'

'Definitely,' agreed Alan Taylor, who was being chased down the beach by violent apes for some reason. 'I've had enough of the seaside.'

*   *   *

And so it was that the three heroes packed up their bags and set off for home. Soon they had left the seaside far behind and were making their way along the winding country lanes. The day was warm and pleasant and the three friends walked in companionable silence as if no words were needed between them to communicate the things they felt.

'No words are needed between us to communicate the things we feel,' said Friday.

The trees twittered and the birds waved gently in the breeze, but as the heroes drew closer to home Polly began to grow uneasy. It was quiet—much too quiet. Something didn't feel right—much too didn't feel right.

'Look,' Polly said, as they came to Old Granny's house on the edge of town. 'Old Granny done pulled her curtains shut. I never seen that before, usually she's far too drunk to remember an' everyone can see her jivin' to her old-fashioned musicals in the lounge.'

All the other houses were just the same. Every one of them stood silent and still. There wasn't a soul to be seen.

It's like a ghost town, thought Polly with a shiver.

Where has everyone disappeared to? thought Alan Taylor with a shiver.

71

Why's everyone shivering? I'd better shiver too, thought Friday with a shiver.

Suddenly—WHOOIMP!—
something sharp and pointy flew through the air. Then—WHOOIMP!—
something else sharp and pointy flew through the air. Then—
K A - F U U U R R R T L E !—

something else sharp and pointy flew through the air.

'I wonder why that last one went "KA-FUUURRRTLE!" instead of "WHOOIMP!"' said Friday O'Leary. 'Isn't life interesting?'

'I'll tell you what else is interesting,' said Alan Taylor, examining the flying

things closely with his knowledgeable raisin eyes. 'These are sheep bones. But what on earth are –'

'DUCK!' yelled Polly as a dead duck came soaring towards them. 'What's a-goin' on in our pretty little town? An' what's that "CHATTER CHATTER CHEE" sound what's scramblin' up my brains like dandelions?'

The frightful noises grew louder as the heroes rounded Boaster's Hill and approached the high street.

'Oh,' said Polly.

'My,' said Alan Taylor.

'Good,' said Friday.

'Lord!' added a helpful passerby to finish the sentence.

Because there it was in all its grisly splendour—the Dinnertime Wars that were tearing the town apart.

'Take that, Greasy Ian!' shouted a scrawny figure who stood in the middle of the high street, lobbing meat wildly in all directions. His clothes were tattered and torn. His cap had gone. His face was covered in scraps of bacon. But Polly recognised him instantly.

74

'Why, it's Billy William the Third!' she gasped. 'But what in the name of Billy William the Third is he ups to? An' who in the name of Greasy Ian is Greasy Ian?'

Suddenly a monstrous fellow covered in boils and chip fat jumped out of an alleyway and began issuing commands.

'Turn the spit, Philip, ma hairy treasure! Turn the spit like ye've never turned it afore!'

'CHATTER CHATTER CHEE!' shrieked a stinky little monkey at his side. And leaping on top of a huge grey kebab the vile creature began cranking the handle for all he was worth.

SPLIP! Hot fat rained down upon the high street. Billy William yelped and went running for cover back to the butcher's shop. But when he opened the door who was lying in wait but . . .

'MR GUM!' shouted Polly, rushing into the midst of the battle without a care for her own safety. 'I knowed you'd be mixed up in all this! Jus' you an' Billy leave that bloke with the monkey alone, you troublemakers!'

'What you on about, you stupid little

girl?' laughed Mr Gum as he swigged on a can of beer. 'Greasy Ian an' the monkey are on my side. It's *Billy* I'm after!'

'Billy?' exclaimed Polly in astonishment. 'But I done thought Billy was your friend, your only friend in the whole wide worlds!'

'Times change, little girl,' growled Mr Gum, brushing her aside like a horse flicking a raisin into space. 'Me an' Greasy Ian's gonna mash Billy up good an' proper.'

'Say yer prayers, Billy me boy!' Mr Gum cackled.

Billy gritted his teeth. There had to be a way out of it. Had to be! But no. It was the end of the line.

In front of him: Mr Gum in his hobnail boots.

Behind him: Greasy Ian with a heavy iron saucepan.

To his left: Philip the Horror with a ladle full of chilli sauce.

To his right: a quite scary ant sitting on the pavement.

Escape was impossible.

The sun had disappeared behind the

clouds. The Kebab Shop Gang were closing in. The ant waved its front leg menacingly.

'We have to stop them!' cried Alan Taylor from Polly's skirt pocket. But before they could think how, a pair of strong hairy monkey arms grabbed them from behind and pinned them tight.

'CHATTER! CHATTER! CHATTER!' shrieked Philip the Horror into Polly's ear.

'Friday! Friday! Help!' shouted Polly, but it was no use. Friday had accidentally fallen asleep in a hedge.

And now Polly and Alan Taylor could only look on as Mr Gum and Greasy Ian advanced on the terrified butcher.

Greasy Ian rolled up his sleeve.

Mr Gum raised his fists.

Philip the Horror bared his yellow teeth.

The ant growled.

'It's all over,' spluttered Alan Taylor, his words muffled beneath the monkey's paw. 'It's the end of society as we know it!'

But no! Hold everything! Stop right there! Because suddenly, every molecule in Polly's body began to tingle as if some marvellous mystical music was playing deep inside her intestines. And into the fray stepped a small boy, a small boy with a face so honest and true that everyone stopped what they were doing and stood rooted to the spot.

'It's the Spirit of the Rainbow!' cried Polly when at last she could speak. 'He's come to end this terrible war onces an' for all!'

CHAPTER NINE

'ONLY LOVE CAN SAVE US NOW'

'Warmongers,' said the Spirit of the Rainbow, gazing upon the villains with his bright clear eyes. He didn't speak loudly but nonetheless it seemed as if the whole world was hanging on every one of his words. 'Warmongers,' he said again. 'Warmongers.'

Then he shook his head sadly and said 'Warmongers' a few more times. It was very dramatic. Also, once he said 'Warmonkeys' instead and he looked right at Philip the Horror that time and Philip the Horror fell silent.

'Warmongers, you have brought fighting and destruction to the streets of this town,' said the Spirit of the Rainbow. 'But now you must turn from your madness. For War is a cruel and heartless mother and her only children are Misery and Bloodshed and Some Explosions. Turn from your madness while there is still a chance. Now leave this place!'

'Shabba me whiskers!' growled Mr Gum—but nonetheless he was afraid of the honesty in that young lad's voice and for now all the fight had gone out of him. 'Come on, Greasy Ian, let's get out of here,' he muttered. 'Not cos I'm

scared of that kid, jus' cos I don't feel like fightin' any more, that's all.'

And so the villains began collecting up their weapons for another day. The Kebab Shop Gang disappeared back to Greasy Ian's by the canal and Billy ~~and his magic unicorn, Elizabeth~~ returned to his butcher's shop to sulk like a rabbit for the rest of the afternoon. The town was silent once more.

*   *   *

'Oh, Spirit, you done it, you done stopped the war!' said Polly, tears of gratitude spilling from her eyes.

'No, child,' said the Spirit of the Rainbow, though he was no older than she. 'The warmongers will be back at it tomorrow—I cannot hold them off forever. War is too strong even for me and my remarkable powers. But there is one force which is stronger still, and that force is called love.'

'But how can love stop this war?' asked Friday O'Leary, scratching the Spirit of the Rainbow's head in puzzlement. 'There's no way I'm kissing Mr Gum, if that's what you're thinking.'

'No,' said the boy solemnly. 'Though I do have a task for you and your friends. You see, Mr Gum and Greasy Ian will never be stopped, for badness flows deep inside their veins. But Billy? I believe Billy can still be turned from this wickedness.'

'But how, Spirit, how?' said Polly.

'Billy is only fighting because he is lonely and jealous,' replied the Spirit of the Rainbow. 'If we can turn his mind to thoughts of love, the fighting will stop and the world will once again glow with happy colours.'

'I sees,' said Polly, nodding slowly. 'So we gots to find Billy a wife.'

'Not just any wife,' said the Spirit of the Rainbow. 'For long ago Billy William pledged his heart to a lady. And ever since that day Billy has lived in hope and now it is time to make that hope come true.'

'But who could Billy William possibly ever love?' asked Friday.

The Spirit of the Rainbow handed Polly a photo.

'*Her? That's* the woman Billy loves?' said Polly in disbelief.

'Billy is a proud man and a smelly one,' replied the boy. 'He could only ever love a butcher as skilful as he. Thora Gruntwinkle is her name. She is the Butcher Queen of Olde London Town.'

'How do you know all this?' asked Alan Taylor, who hadn't said anything for a while.

'Some of it is written in the stars,' replied the young lad, gazing into the distance as if seeing things there that mere mortals could not. 'Some of it has been foretold in the mighty Prophecies of Bastos. And some of it I just make up as I go along. Enough questions! You must travel to London and do not tarry!'

'I don't suppose you'd like to come with us?' said Friday hopefully.

'No, my friend Colin's having a bowling party tonight,' said the strange boy. 'Now go! The next train leaves on the hour. Bring back Thora Gruntwinkle—before it is too late!'

And throwing them a handful of fruit chews he was gone.

CHAPTER ONE

MEET MR FLAMINGO

Hello. Do you know who I am? I do, because I'm me. I'm Mr Flamingo and I'm absolutely splendid. Guess how many fish I can catch in one day? LOADS. Also, look at my beak, it's tremendous. And if that weren't already enough look how brilliant I am at standing on one leg. It's no wonder everyone around here thinks I'm superb—I am. The other thing is, I'm very pink and what do you think of that? I think it's marvellous. Do you know why I'm so pink? It's because of all the little shrimps I'm eating all day. The little shrimps have got strange chemicals in them which make them pink and those strange chemicals make my feathers pink too. Isn't that something?

Also, have you met my wife? Her name is Mrs Flamingo and she is very attractive. All the other flamingos totally wanted to marry her but I soon put a stop to that by kicking them into the water and jumping up and down on them until they knew who was the boss. Then, after everyone knew who was the boss (me), I went up to Mrs Flamingo and I said, 'See who is the strongest and the most attractive? It is me.' And Mrs Flamingo (who was just called Miss Flamingo back then) agreed and soon we were married in the Church of the Golden Hippopotamus down by the mudflats. It's great being married, you should try it some time. We've been married for nearly nine years now and in all that time we've hardly ever argued. And we've got two lovely children, Michael and Penny.

So anyway, now you've met my family it's time to tell you of the time the rhino came to town. It was a lazy Saturday afternoon and I was idly preening my beautiful feathers when

Dear Readers,

We have just been informed of a disastrous printing error in 'What's For Dinner, Mr Gum?' Apparently thousands and thousands of copies have been mistakenly printed with a chapter about a flamingo instead of a chapter about going to London on a train. If you have been the victim of one of these 'flamingo-y' copies, please visit: **www.egmont.co.uk/missingchapter** where you can read the correct chapter as nature intended.

Yours Sincerely,

Mr Egmont

Mr Egmont, the Publisher

Mrs Egmont

And his wife, Mrs Egmont*

*Still just Mr Egmont wearing a dress

Chapter Eleven

OLDE LONDON TOWN

'I never done beened in a big city before,' said Polly as they stepped off the platform into the crowded railway station. 'Look at all the shops! There must be at leasts six of them.'

'And that's just in the station,' replied Friday, who was a great traveller. 'In actual fact, there are over THIRTY shops in the whole of London and that is why it is known as "The Shopper's Paradise". You can buy anything in London, Polly. Anything you want! Anything you can imagine! Anything at all!'

'But can you buy happiness?' said Alan Taylor quietly and that made them all think for a moment.

*   *   *

'WELCOME TO LONDON!' yelled the Queen as Polly and her friends stepped out of the station and straight on to a busy street crowded with pedestrians, pigeons, punks, parking meters, policemen, policewomen, pussycats, ponies, pubs, pushbikes, pushchairs, prams, payphones, pickpockets, pop stars, paparazzi, postmen, pies, puppies, paupers, pavement artists, potholes, puddles, priests, poodles and just to ruin everything, an onion.

'What a marveller it all is,' said Polly, her eyes goggling as she gazed upon the many sights and sounds, even though you can't really gaze upon sounds. 'Can we goes to Piccalilli Circus an' see the clowns?'

'There's no time for that,' said Alan Taylor, who was sitting in Polly's hair so he wouldn't be trodden on by a businessman or eaten by a Beefeater for dessert. 'We've got to find Thora Gruntwinkle and I think I know where she might be.'

'You do?' said Friday O'Leary in surprise.

'I certainly do,' said Alan Taylor. 'Do you remember

what I was like when you first met me?'

'I remembers,' said Polly. 'You was a horrid little richie with far too much money for your own goods. You was always splashin' it about an' showin' off like nobody's fat business.'

'That's right, Polly,' said Alan Taylor. 'But have you ever wondered just how I came to have all that money in the first place?'

'No,' said Friday.

'You see,' explained Alan Taylor, 'I used to work right here in Olde London Town! I was a taxi driver and I know this city like the back of my tasty little hand. Now, if we're *very* lucky . . .' he said, scanning the street with his bright raisin eyes. 'Yes! There it is!'

Suddenly, to Polly's astonishment Alan Taylor somersaulted from her hair and began running pell mell down Pall Mall, dodging amongst the legs of the pedestrians and chortling with glee.

'What's got into him?' said Friday. But it wasn't what had got into Alan Taylor, it was what had Alan Taylor got into—a dusty old black taxi cab with a crumpled bonnet, a couple of flat tyres and hundreds of parking tickets plastered all over the windscreen.

'My old taxi!' cried Alan Taylor, bouncing up and down on the front seat with such gusto that the whole street stopped to stare. 'Right where I left it three years ago—parked in front of this "NO PARKING" sign. What a stroke of luck! Hop in!' he called. 'Hop in!'

Polly and Friday hopped in.

'To the Butcher's District!' proclaimed Alan Taylor. He turned the ignition key and—*SMUNF!*—they were off!

Of course, a London taxi cab is very big and Alan Taylor was very small so he kept having to jump down from the steering wheel to press the pedals. And then, every now and again when he remembered, he'd jump back up to turn the steering wheel by dancing on it, his little legs whizzing up and down and his electric muscles buzzing like a toaster about to explode. He seemed to be having so much fun that Polly couldn't help but laugh through her terror.

'He's a-goin' to kill us!' she giggled as the oncoming traffic swerved to get out of their way. 'He's a-goin' to kill us all!' The other drivers honked their horns or shouted 'BEEP BEEP!' Crowds of shoppers ducked for cover as the cab skidded on to the pavement, knocking over an ice-cream stand and one of those stalls that sell useless souvenirs of London like plastic Big Bens and postcards of idiotic-looking punks.

'LOOK OUT! LOOK OUT!' the cry went up. 'ALAN TAYLOR'S BACK IN TOWN!'

'How on earth did you become rich driving like *this*?' yelled Friday as Alan Taylor accidentally ran over Sherlock Holmes and hurt his foot.

'My passengers used to pay me double to let them out of the cab almost as soon as they'd got in,' replied Alan Taylor, bouncing happily up and down on the accelerator. 'I made lots of money that way.'

'Look!' shouted Polly as they

whizzed past the famous sights of the nation's capital. 'An old chestnut-seller dyin' of the plague! Mary Poppins beatin' up a tramp! Chimney sweeps a-dancin' all over Nelson's Column! Dr Jekyll turnin' into a pigeon! Isn't it grand, Friday, isn't it grand!'

'CROPPER IN THE FLOPPER!' agreed Friday, who occasionally liked to say 'CROPPER IN THE FLOPPER!' instead of 'yes'.

Suddenly Alan Taylor jumped down on the brake as hard as he could. With an awful smell of burning rubber and gingerbread, the taxi spun round and round in the middle of the road. The front wheel bounced off, flew into the Houses of Parliament and accidentally became Prime Minister for the next ten years. The engine fell out and rolled into the River Thames . . . And then all was still.

'B-b-where are we?' said Polly, looking dazedly around.

'We're lost,' said Friday.

'No, we're not,' smiled Alan Taylor, pointing to the old-fashioned street sign on the corner:

CARVER'S ROW

'All of London's butchers live and work on Carver's Row,' he explained. 'If Thora Gruntwinkle's anywhere in this crazy city then this is where we'll find her.'

*　　*　　*

What a horrible street of meat Carver's Row turned out to be. It was a place of unwashed windows and broken doorways. It was a place of plucked geese and wild-eyed hares dangling

from hooks of cruel black steel. It was a place of surly fat men sitting on wooden crates drinking beer, huge meat cleavers dangling from their aprons and smaller meat cleavers dangling from

their socks. It was a place of butchers.

'I'm scared,' whispered Polly, but Alan Taylor took her hand and that gave her the courage to go forward. And Friday took her foot and that gave her the courage to trip over and say, 'Friday, please stop taking my foot.'

'Keep your eyes straight ahead, Polly,' muttered Friday. 'And keep smiling. Butchers can smell fear, you know. It's one of their powers.'

'Spare some change for a cuppa tea?' whined a wretched beggar at Polly's feet—but Alan Taylor pulled Polly briskly away.

'Don't give him any money,' he warned. 'He'll only spend it on kidneys and mince.'

Strange eyes watched the heroes from dark doorways. Sharp silver blades flashed and flickered in the shadows. A miserable butcher's dog snuffled for scraps in the gutters.

'MEEAATT! FREESSHH MEEAAAT!' bubbled a low-pitched voice from behind a boarded-up window.

'BEEF BRISKET! GET YER BEEF BRISKET!' growled another.

'CANDYFLOSS AN' TOFFEE APPLES!' cried a third. 'CANDYFLOSS AN'– oops, sorry. I think I'm in the wrong street.'

At last the heroes came to the very last shop on Carver's Row.

GRUNTWINKLE'S
QUALITY CUTS

Fine meats and poultry,
whatever poultry is

The sun was going down behind the sooty brick buildings, sinking like a great bloody eye into the blackness. The evening had grown cold. From one of the neighbouring buildings there came the dull sound of a meat cleaver coming down, over and over again.

'Well,' Polly said softly. The door loomed over her, tall and dark and ominous. 'Here we goes then.'

Polly glanced round at her friends. She took a deep breath. And then she stepped through the doorway.

Chapter Twelve

THORA GRUNTWINKLE

'Good evening!' called a lovely musical voice, and Thora Gruntwinkle stepped out from behind the counter to greet them.

'My goodness,' marvelled Friday. 'She's even more beautiful in real life than in her photo!'

And so she was. No photograph could ever do justice to the beauty of Thora Gruntwinkle for she was one of the most gorgeous ladies who ever was born, like an angel who wasn't looking where it was going, tripped over a comet and plummeted to Earth to walk prettily amongst us for the rest of its days. Her auburn hair, her emerald eyes, her radiant smile—she was breathtaking.

'Pity about her name though,' whispered Friday.

Thora Gruntwinkle's shop was just as beautiful as she, with a spotless white counter and a pretty display of plump pheasants and partridges hanging above.

Gleaming pink cuts of gammon and ham sat side by side in a sparkling glass case and indeed, wherever you looked, there were fabulous meats to behold. Lamb cutlets, rich dark venison, thick juicy slabs of sirloin steak ... All in all it was a splendid place, and it just goes to show: Never judge a butcher by the cover.

'What can I do for you lovely people today?' beamed Thora Gruntwinkle. 'We've got some absolutely *wonderful* French hens—all free-range and organic, of course.'

'Oh, Miss Gruntwinkle,' said Polly, 'we din't come in search of your delicious an' hygienic meat products, we done come here cos there's a 'mergency goin' on in Lamonic Bibber.'

And so Polly explained all about the Dinnertime Wars. It took nearly two

minutes to tell the whole tale but Thora listened patiently all the while, nodding from time to time to show she was paying attention rather than just standing there not saying stuff.

'Oh, dear,' she frowned when the sad story was done. 'I'm very sorry for you all but what can I possibly do to— MAN ALIVE! WHAT ON EARTH'S THAT THING IN YOUR HAIR?!'

'Oh, that's just Alan Taylor,' laughed Polly. 'He's a gingerbread man with 'lectric muscles.'

'Well, I never,' laughed Thora Gruntwinkle, shaking the tiny fellow by the hand. 'Sorry for yelling, Mr Taylor, I've never met anyone so small and impossible before.'

'That's all right,' grinned Alan Taylor, his electric muscles sparking merrily. 'Now where were we?'

'Oh, yeah,' said Polly. 'Miss Gruntwinkle, sir, we needs you to come back with us to Lamonic Bibber.'

'Me?' said Thora Gruntwinkle. 'But why?'

'It's cos Billy William's well in love with you,' explained Polly. 'An' we reckons that if you goes an' fall in love with him too then he'll stop all his lonely angers an' the war will be over.'

'I see,' said Thora, smiling wider than they'd ever seen her smile before, which wasn't that amazing as they'd only known her for about ten minutes. 'Well, I have always longed to get out of Carver's Row and find a nice place to settle down, away from all the bustle and smoke. But tell me about this "Billy" gentleman. What's he like? Is he handsome and delightful?'

Friday, Polly and Alan Taylor looked at each other guiltily.

'Um . . .' began Polly.

'Oh, what have I got to lose?' trilled Thora. 'Let's go!'

'YES!' cried Polly triumphantly.

'YES!' cried Alan Taylor.

'CROPPER IN THE FLOPPER!' cried Friday. 'To the train station! We're going home!'

CHAPTER THIRTEEN

THE HEROES RETURN. AGAIN.
PLUS THERE'S ONE MORE OF
THEM THIS TIME

'Wake up,' said Friday to himself to
wake himself up. 'Wake up, Friday,
we're nearly there.'

Friday awoke with a yawn and
looked out the train window. They'd
been travelling all night but now the
sun was rising over the sea, dazzling in
its glory, like the biggest grapefruit
imaginable emerging from its nest to
hunt for sugar.

'Rise and shine, friends,' said Friday,
kicking and punching the others with
his mind until they awoke. 'We're
here.'

'Already?' yawned Polly, climbing
carefully down from the overhead
luggage compartment. Alan Taylor
poked his head out of her skirt pocket,
blinked twice and went back to sleep.
He'd seen it all before. But after a life

spent in grey Olde London Town, Thora Gruntwinkle could hardly believe it.

'Oh, it's glorious,' she gasped, as the sparkling blue ocean sped by outside the window. 'I've never seen the sea before.'

'How do you know it's the sea then?' said Friday suspiciously. 'Are you a SPY?'

'No, I just guessed,' said Thora Gruntwinkle innocently, and Friday relaxed once more.

Now the train was pulling into Lamonic Bibber's cheerful little station—but what was this? The opposite platform was bustling with townsfolk, all of them with suitcases and trunks piled high.

Old Granny was there with her sherry cabinet from before the War. Beany McLeany, who loved things that rhymed, was standing there with a rubber doll, a barber's pole and a cheese and sun-dried tomato roll. Martin Launderette, who ran the launderette, was there with his launderette. Somehow he'd managed to

put it on wheels, who even knows how? Jonathan Ripples, the fattest man in town, was there with his fridge. Henrietta Unimportant was there but never mind her. The Invisible Twins were there—or maybe they weren't. It was hard to tell.

And every one of them had an anxious expression on his or her face. Except possibly the Invisible Twins. It was hard to tell.

*   *   *

'Hey!' cried Polly, crossing over to the other platform. 'Where you all goin' with your bags an' your cases an' your portable laund'rettes?'

'Why, haven't you heard, Polly?' said Jonathan Ripples, chewing on Beany McLeany's cheese roll when he wasn't looking. 'There's a war on. We're all getting out of Lamonic Bibber.'

'Yes, it's not safe here,' hiccuped Old Granny, who was quite drunk. 'We're off to find a new town to live in. One without wars going on.'

Polly shook her head in disbelief.

'**Townsfolk**,' she exclaimed, 'I simply cannot believes what cowards you done turned yourselves into. Me an' my friends gone all the way to Olde London Town to save the day. We sat through Alan Taylor's 'trocious drivin', we braved the terrors of Carver's Row—but if you can't even be bothered to stick around I doesn't even think this town's worth savin' in the first place.'

'Oh, really, Polly?' sneered Martin Launderette. 'And just how *were* you planning to save the town anyway?'

'I'm not tellin' the likes of you, sir,' said Polly. 'If anyone wants to come an' see for theirselves that's up to them. But if you wants to jus' hop on a great big train an' turn your wriggly backs on Lamonic Bibber then good lucks an' good mornin' to you all, says I.'

And she crossed back over the platform to rejoin her friends.

'Nicely put, Polly,' said Friday.

'Well,' shrugged Polly, 'they're jus' a load of Jimmy-Spinners what don't even knows how to stick up for the Forces of Good. Now come on,' she said to Thora Gruntwinkle. 'We gotta gets you to that battlefield an' turn it into a lovefield 'fore it's too late.'

CHAPTER FOURTEEN

THE POWER OF LOVE

'CHATTER CHATTER CHEE!'
BANG! BANG!
KA-THING!
WHOOOOOOOOSHHH!
'OUCH!'

Kebab meat and entrails whizzed through the air as the heroes approached the high street.

'It's worse than ever,' said Polly. 'I can't hardly see nothin' through this smoke.'

'Who said that?' said Friday.

'CHATTER CHATTER CHEE!'
'OW! ME LEG!'

KA-BLLLLAMMM!

'And who's that over there?' said Thora Gruntwinkle, pointing to a figure in the smog.

'It's Billy William,' whispered Polly. 'Do you loves him yet?' she asked hopefully.

'I'm not sure, it's hard to make him out properly,' replied Thora G.

As they came closer the full scale of the war became apparent. Meat was spattered everywhere, the houses were all boarded up and as for Billy William's Right Royal Meats, well, it no longer resembled a butcher's shop at all. Billy had turned it into a fortress with turrets and barricades and a drawbridge with his own face painted on the door. And high up on the parapet stood Billy himself, ready to defend his castle from attack.

He had a cannon and everything. Well, actually he didn't have everything. But he did have a cannon, that much is true.

'Come out an' show yourselves!' he cried to his enemies now. And lighting the cannon's fuse with a flaming hot chicken wing he blasted a lump of goat meat straight into the middle of the high street.

'Come out an' show yourselves, you pathetic crisps!'

'Oh, don't you worry, we will!' shouted Mr Gum from somewhere off in the distance. This was followed by some horrible laughter. And then silence, a heavy silence which hung in the air like the end of worlds.

'Uh oh,' said Friday. 'Something bad's going to happen. I can just tell.'

SHHMMMMMUFFFF!

A rumbling, lumbering noise, faint at first but growing by the minute.

SHHHHHMMMMUUFUFFF!
SHUUMMMUFUFFUFUFF!
SHHMMMMUFUFUFUFUF!

'I knew it,' gasped Friday, courageously hiding behind Alan Taylor. 'This is bad!'

The ground cracked and groaned

and trembled as the noise grew until it seemed as if that was it—the whole place would just split apart like Jonathan Ripples' shirt after one too many ice creams.

SHHSHSHHHMMMMUFFUF!

From out of the smoke it came. A monstrous, hollowed-out kebab, a kebab as big as a tank. Dripping grease and oozing oil by the gallon it lurched slowly forward. In some places it was brown, in others grey. In still others it was blackened and burnt and as hard as iron and steel. And it stank so bad even the baying hounds who followed in its wake were afraid to get any nearer.

The ultimate fighting machine.
The engine of destruction.
The KEBABILATOR.
There was a hatch at the front and through that hatch Polly saw a sight she would never forget in all her days. Greasy Ian. Mr Gum. And Philip the Horror. Which was man and which was beast?

Polly could not tell, for their eyes all blazed with the madness of war and it was the most terrifying thing she had ever seen, even including the bit in that film where all those toy clowns come to life and start dancing around on the table.

'You got no chance this time, Billy der Willy der Wills!' roared Mr Gum, his teeth gnashing and his beard flying behind him like wildfire. 'We're gonna smash you to pieces with our greases!'

'Faster, Philip, faster!' urged Greasy Ian, waving his big brass fist. Philip the Horror turned the handle and the Kebabilator rumbled forward.

'FIVE!' shouted Mr Gum as they approached the butcher's shop.

'FOUR!' bellowed Greasy Ian.

'CHATTER CHATTER CHEE!' screamed Philip the Horror.

'TWO!' shouted Mr Gum.

Billy was frantically reloading his cannon but even a fool could see he was out of time.

'He's out of time,' said Friday O'Leary.

Any moment now the Kebabilator would smash Billy's fort to bits.

But now Polly seemed to hear a voice inside her heart, the pure true voice of the Spirit of the Rainbow, reminding her of what had to be done.

'Only love can save us now,' said the voice. *'Shove Thora into the middle of things and see what happens.'*

So Polly shoved Thora Gruntwinkle into the middle of things.

There the beautiful vision stood, Mr Gum's war machine on one side, Billy and his cannon on the other.

As if awaking from a trance Philip the Horror stopped turning the handle.

Slowly the Kebabilator rumbled to a halt.

Billy put down the cannon.

Thora stared at the villains.

The villains stared back at her.

Time seemed to stand still.

And then . . .

Their eyes met across the crowded battlefield.

Somewhere in the distance a string quartet started to play.

Everything went all slow-motion.

'It's the power of love,' whispered Friday in amazement.

'Yes,' said Alan Taylor unnecessarily.

'Thooooooooooooraaaaaaaaa!' exclaimed Billy. 'Yoooou caaaaame for meeeeee!'

Billy scrambled down from his fortress and ran for Thora Gruntwinkle. She was no longer just a

poster on his wall, she was really here!
He threw his arms out wide to get his
hands on the love. Thora started
running too.

The string music swelled.

Billy ran faster.

Thora ran faster still.

'My love!' cried Billy William the
Third.

'My darling!' cried Thora
Gruntwinklc.

But Thora Gruntwinkle wasn't
running towards Billy.

'You're just who I've been searching
for!' said Thora Gruntwinkle, throwing
herself into the brawny arms of Greasy
Ian. 'You're big and strong <u>and</u> you've
got a pet monkey! Oh, Greasy Ian!' she
said, guessing his name instantly, which
is always how it happens when you
meet your one true love. 'Will you
marry me?'

'Aye,' nodded Greasy Ian and they
put their lips together and started
slurping away at each other, just like at
the end of a film.

'Shabba me whiskers!' muttered Mr
Gum. 'I think I'm gonna be sick.'

'BLEURGH,' agreed Billy William the Third.

And that was it.

Confetti just came down from nowhere, no one even knows why. Bluebirds appeared, cheering everyone up through not one but two methods:

1/ Chirping
2/ Eating the scraps of old meat that were lying in the road

And the sun came out and the clouds blew away and the Kebabilator was carried off by squirrels and recycled into delicious acorns. And far, far away in Carver's Row, a single daisy pushed its way up through the cracks in the cobblestones and sat there blinking proudly in the sunshine.

*   *   *

Yes, my friends, it was the power of love and it couldn't ever be stopped, not even in a thousand years. Not even in a million years. Not even in a million million years. Well, maybe in a million

million years, but who cares? You and I won't be around then anyway. Especially me.

But hey, sorry. Don't think about that. Think about the power of love, which makes life worth living in the first place. For without love what is there? Just a lot of homework and sitting around watching bad TV.

CHAPTER FIFTEEN

ALL'S WELL THAT ENDS GOOD

'Hooray,' said Polly. 'The nightmare is over an' the world can dream happy dreamers again.'

'I could not have put it better, child,' said a familiar voice and Polly spun around—but the Spirit of the Rainbow was already gone, leaving behind only the tinkling of his laughter and a handful of fruit chews lying 'pon the roadside.

'Amazing,' said Alan Taylor, shaking his head in awe.

'Will we ever sees him again?' wondered Polly.

'Who knows, little miss, who knows?' said Friday, gazing into the distance. And the sun warmed their faces and the fresh wind cheered their souls and together the heroes stood there for some time, thinking about how mysterious and wonderful and good life could be. Except for Friday, who was mostly thinking he quite fancied a yogurt.

*　　　*　　　*

'But what 'bouts all them townsfolk who deserted Lamonic Bibber in its greatest hour of need?' said Polly at length.

'I don't think we need worry about that,' laughed Alan Taylor. 'Look behind you, Polly, look!'

So Polly did, and how overjoyed was she to see all the townsfolk walking back to town, their suitcases forgotten? Very overjoyed.

'You comed back!' she exclaimed in her perfect English. 'You never done left us after all!'

'How could we get on that train after your inspiring words, Polly?' beamed big-hearted, big-stomached Jonathan Ripples. 'You talked sense into our traitorous heads and reminded us of the town we truly love.'

And with that they all joined their arms together and sang a cheerful song called 'Can Someone Please Untangle

Our Arms? They've Got Stuck'.

'Oh, what a friendly town this is,' laughed Thora Gruntwinkle. 'It's just as I hoped.'

'Chatter chatter chee,' agreed Philip the Horror politely, taking hold of Thora's pretty hand.

'Look, all he needed was a mother,' smiled Friday. 'Now he's the nicest monkey in the world. Or at least in the top twenty.'

'An' that's it,' said Polly contentedly. 'All's well that ends good. The story's over.'

'No, my friend,' said Greasy Ian and already Polly could see how love was making him a kinder man and slightly taller. 'The story has just begun. Me an' Thora's gettin' married in ten minutes an' you're all invited. There'll be roses an' music an' the fattest feast money can buy. But I promise—no kebabs shall there be. Those days are over!'

'THE TRUTH IS A LEMON MERINGUE!' cried Friday O'Leary. 'To the Wedding Gardens, everyone! To the Wedding Gardens!'

And so, laughing and singing and

cavorting, everyone headed off to the Wedding Gardens to see Thora Gruntwinkle and Greasy Ian married in the sunshine. Polly, Alan Taylor, Old Granny, big-hearted Jonathan Ripples, Martin Launderette— everyone!
Well, almost everyone.

'I ain't going to no stupid flippin' weddin' business,' scowled Mr Gum as the townsfolk skipped off. 'Shabba me whiskers! What a dirty rotten bother the whole thing is!'

'I ain't goin' neither,' said Billy William the Third, spitting into a molehill to annoy whatever might be

down there, most likely a mole.

'Love—who needs it? No one, that's who.'

'Well, then,' said Mr Gum. 'Seems like we been left all on our own again, don't it?'

'Yeah,' said Billy, avoiding Mr Gum's eye.

'Yeah,' said Mr Gum, examining a passing cloud as if it interested him greatly.

'OK, then,' said Billy. 'Well, I'll see ya around, Mr Gum.'

'Yeah,' said Mr Gum. 'OK. See ya around, Billy.'

'Bye then.'

'Bye.'

The two men turned and began walking, Billy back to his half-ruined butcher's shop and Mr Gum to his lonesome old house where the only company he had was the mice and the insects and the black and white TV with the dodgy homemade aerial. But before they'd gone very far Mr Gum suddenly spun around.

'Um, Billy me boy,' said Mr Gum awkwardly.

'What is it, Mr Gum, me old letter-box?' said Billy, stopping in his tracks.

'You thinkin' what I'm thinkin'?' said Mr Gum.

'Maybe,' said Billy William. 'I'm thinkin' 'bout goin' down to the Old Meadow to find some new pet flies.'

'Nah, you can do that anytime,' said Mr Gum. 'What I was thinkin' was this: how 'bout you an' me go to that weddin' after all an' sit in the back ruinin' it for everyone by makin' loud fartin' noises?'

'Now yer talkin',' grinned Billy.

'Come on, Billy me old best friend,' said Mr Gum, affectionately punching Billy William in the belly as hard as he possibly could.

'We got scoundrel plans to make an' people to annoy!'

'Let's start with Philip the Horror,' said Billy as they walked on up the road.

'Yeah,' scowled Mr Gum. 'CHATTER CHATTER CHEE! CHATTER CHATTER CHEE! all day long. Between you an' me, Billy—I never could stand that monkey.'

THE END

WHAT, NO JAKE THE DOG?

Come on, you didn't think we'd leave Jake out of this book altogether, did you? Of COURSE we wouldn't, for as they say in Lamonic Bibber:

A book without Jake is like a snake without a snake.

So here he is right now, starring in his very own **SUPER BONUS STORY**, that massive whopper of a dog, weighing in at nearly two hundred pounds, the one, the only, JAKE THE DOG in . . .

JAKE GETS A JOB

Now, it sometimes happened that Jake the dog would take himself for a morning stroll through the woods to look for biscuits and that is where this story begins. It was the kind of morning that is nice. There was some weather in the sky and it wasn't the cold, wet kind, it was the other kind with all the heat and bright light. Just the sort of a day for a massive whopper of a dog to go strolling through the woods looking for biscuits, wouldn't you agree?

Yes.

But as Jake went snuzzling amongst the trees and flowers, who should happen to see him but a rich American businessman called Ray Mozzarella.

Now, Ray Mozzarella always wore sunglasses, even when he was indoors, even in the bath, even in bed, and even on the toilet. In fact, especially on the toilet. And even if there was a big sign saying 'ANYONE WEARING

SUNGLASSES WILL BE ARRESTED AND EATEN ALIVE BY CRANES' it wouldn't stop Ray Mozzarella. He'd just carry on wearing his sunglasses. He thought it looked cool.

'OHO,' said Ray Mozzarella when he saw Jake the dog strolling by, barking like a witch-chaser. 'Look at this dude! He's just the guy to run my big important company.'

You see, what with those sunglasses on, Ray Mozzarella couldn't tell Jake was just a dog.

'Hey, dude,' said Ray Mozzarella. 'How d'ya fancy running my company for me?'

'WOOF,' said Jake.

'I can't understand a word you Brits say,' said Ray Mozzarella. 'But I love your accent. You're hired!'

And the next thing Jake knew, he was in a jet plane flying across the Atlantic Ocean.

'Guess you must be real excited about coming to work for my important company, huh?' called Ray Mozzarella from the cockpit.

'WOOF,' said Jake, who was busy searching for biscuits under the seats.

'Thought so,' said Ray Mozzarella, landing the jet in the Statue of Liberty's left nostril. Yes, they had arrived in New York, New York, so good they named it twice. And if you think it wasn't full of skyscrapers you'd be so wrong it's unbelievable.

It was absolutely STUFFED with skyscrapers, all of them stretching towards the heavens like giant shiny schoolchildren putting up their hands to answer a question from their teacher, Mr Sky.

'Right,' said Ray Mozzarella. 'You see that skyscraper over there that's just a bit taller than all the rest? Well, that is where you'll be working. Your office is right at the top on the 200th floor. Whaddya think of that?'

'WOOF,' said Jake.

'Thought so,' said Ray Mozzarella, who still couldn't understand Jake's British accent. So up they zoomed in the elevator to the 200th floor. And there Jake was shown to a black leather chair behind a huge desk overlooking the whole of Manhattan, so good they named it once.

'OK, this job's real simple but real important,' said Ray Mozzarella. 'All you gotta do is pick up the phone when it rings and shout big numbers at whoever's calling. That's what business is all about, but hey, why am I telling you all this? You know it already.'

'WOOF,' said Jake.

'Exactly,' said Ray Mozzarella. 'Now, about your pay. How does one hundred thousand dollars an hour sound?'

'WOOF,' said Jake.

'Not enough, huh?' said Ray Mozzarella. 'OK, two hundred thousand.'

'WOOF,' said Jake again.

'OK, three hundred thousand it is,' said Ray Mozzarella. 'Right, see you later, I have to meet the President for lunch and I'm already eight days late.'

*   *   *

Jake spent the rest of the morning

trying to get the desk drawer open in case there were any biscuits inside. He had almost succeeded when suddenly— BRNG! BRNG!—the phone started ringing. Jake looked at the phone curiously.

BRNG! BRNG! said the phone.

'WOOF!' said Jake.

BRNG! BRNG! said the phone.

Jake turned his attention back to the desk drawer.

*   *   *

BRNG! BRNG!
BRNG! BRNG!
BRNG! BRNG!

All afternoon the phone had been ringing solidly as the important businessmen tried to get through. But by now Jake had dug up most of the carpet looking for biscuits and was sound asleep in a puddle of his own dribble, dreaming of a lovely poodle he fancied.

At the end of the day Ray Mozzarella

came back in. 'How was your first day, champ?' he said. But there was no answer.

'Uh-oh,' said Ray Mozzarella. For the first time since he'd been born he whipped off his sunglasses. There was no one in the office.

'Uh-oh,' said Ray Mozzarella. He went over to the desk. The light on the phone's answering machine was flashing.

*** 4,000 UNPLAYED MESSAGES ***

No one had picked up the phone all day.

'4,000 UNPLAYED MESSAGES!' screamed Ray Mozzarella. 'I'M RUINED! I ain't got a nickel! I ain't got a dime! I'm COMPLETELY RUINED!'

But what did Jake know of all this? Nothing. He had wandered out on to the streets of New York and was playing with the pigeons in Times Square. Eventually a kindly policeman found him and shoved him on a boat back to England. And two days later he was back in Lamonic Bibber, barking like a fatty as if nothing had happened.

'Jakey!' said Polly when she saw him. 'Where you been all week? Everythin's gone well crazy while you been away!'

'Yes,' said Friday O'Leary, showing Jake the newspaper. 'Look, New York's lost all its money because someone didn't pick up a phone or something. And now, guess what? The whole WORLD's lost all its money—just because some lazy business guy couldn't be bothered to answer the phone! What do you think of that then, Jake?'

'Don't be silly, Frides,' said Polly, ruffling Jake's soft golden fur. 'Jakey don't know what you're talkin' 'bout. He don't understand businesses an' moneys an' offices where they make all them important decisions. He's only a dog, after all.'

And she reached into her skirt pocket and brought out a biscuit.

'WOOF,' said Jake happily. It was good to be back home.

ABOUT THE AUTHOR

Andy Stanton lives in North London. He studied English at Oxford but they kicked him out. He has been a film script reader, a cartoonist, an NHS lackey and lots of other things. He has many interests, but best of all he likes cartoons, books and music (even jazz). One day he'd like to live in New York or Berlin or one of those places because he's got fantasies of bohemia. His favourite expression is 'When you are crying, bees sting you' and his favourite word is 'Splarshington!' This is his sixth book.

ABOUT THE ILLUSTRATOR

David Tazzyman lives in South London with his girlfriend, Melanie, and their son, Stanley.

He grew up in Leicester, studied illustration at Manchester Metropolitan University and then travelled around Asia for three years before moving to London in 1997. He likes football, cricket, biscuits, music and drawing. He still dislikes celery.